W9-CFX-269

ABDO Publishing Company is the exclusive school and library distributor of Rabbit Ears Books.

Library bound edition 2006.

Library of Congress Cataloging-in-Publication Data

Gleeson, Brian.
  The tiger and the Brahmin / written by Brian Gleeson ; illustrated by Kurt Vargö.
     p. cm.
  "Rabbit Ears books."
  Summary: A Brahmin deceived by a hungry tiger is saved by a lowly jackal and encounters a lesson he has never found in his holy books.
  ISBN 1-59679-347-3
  [1. Folklore—India.] I. Vargö, Kurt, ill. II. Title.

PZ8.1.G4594Ti 2005
398.2 0954—dc22
[E]

                                                            2004066347

All Rabbit Ears books are reinforced library binding
and manufactured in the United States of America.

The Tiger and the Brahmin

Written by Brian Gleeson

Illustrated by Kurt Vargö

Rabbit Ears Books

There is a land in the East, called India. It is a magical and mysterious place, and the customs of the people who live there may seem strange to an outsider. ✷ In India, everyone has a duty. The animals, too, have their duties. ✷ The rooster crows at dawn to wake the people of the village. The farmer tills his fields so that the crops may grow and the people will have something to eat. The cow gives milk for nourishment. The weaver makes the khadi cloth by spinning at her wheel so that the people may have clothes to wear. The mongoose protects the people by catching the deadly cobra. The shepherd boy minds his goats so that they will grow strong and bear kids. And the merchant sells his wares at the bazaar so that he can drink tea and learn everyone's business. ✷ These are the ancient laws by which the people of India live. For in India, all things have a purpose.

T here was once a wise and holy man in India, a Brahmin. He was a good man who always acquired merit by performing helpful deeds for the people of his village.

✿ When a beggar asked for food, the Brahmin gave food to the poor wretch. When two men quarreled, the Brahmin made peace. When a villager required counseling, the Brahmin consulted the heavens and gave advice that rang true. ✿ If you were to ask the Brahmin why he always performed good deeds, he would reply: "Because that is my duty. My duty is to ease suffering through compassion. It is my responsibility to fulfill my duty." ✿ The Brahmin was a most remarkable fellow, bringing goodness and wisdom wherever he went.

ne day, the Brahmin heard sobbing from under the shadow of a mango tree. He went to see who it was that cried. The Brahmin was astonished to discover a tiger trapped in a cage. ❂ The tiger wailed in the presence of the Brahmin: "Oh, help me, holy one. Please let me out of the cage, Brahmin Babu. If you don't I shall be killed and skinned for some Sahib's rug." ❂ Now, the tiger's request presented a most curious problem for the Brahmin. You see, according to his holy scriptures, it was his duty to practice charity to all things great and small. But if he freed the tiger from the cage, the Brahmin might very well become the tiger's dinner. ❂ "Tiger," said the Brahmin. "I would very much like to help thee, however if I do such a thing I am liable to be eaten. All of India knows that the tiger has a most voracious appetite."

❂ "I give you assurances," cried the tiger. "I shan't eat you if you let me out of the cage. I shall repay your kindness with graditude. I swear to Vishnu that I won't eat you." ❂ The Brahmin hesitated for a moment. ❂ "Tiger appears most righteous," thought the Brahmin. "He is in dire straits and I must assist him."

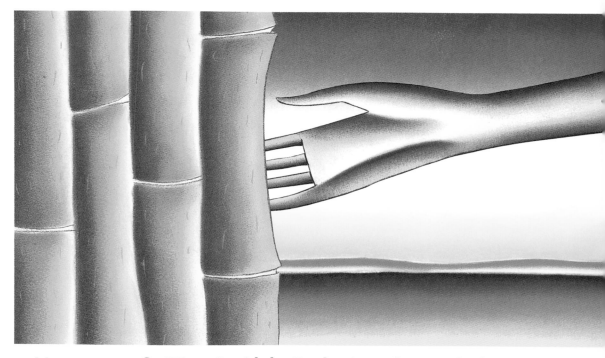

❂ "Tiger," said the Brahmin. "The Hand of Friendship shall avert the Cage of Calamity. I shall set you free!" ❂ With that the Brahmin opened the door to the cage.

The tiger immediately bounded out of his confinement and pounced on the unsuspecting Brahmin. He quickly wrestled the holy man to the ground and took hold of his throat. ✺ "What a fool thou art, Brahmin," he roared loudly. "You believed that drivel about repaying your kindness with my gratitude. Even an imbecile knows that the tiger never lets his dinner walk away." ✺ The Brahmin was petrified. "Mine end is here," he thought. ✺ "Oh tiger," said the Brahmin. "I was kind enough to give you your freedom. Thou repays my freedom thus? Surely, this is not a just reward." ✺ "What would you have me do?" replied the Tiger. "It is my duty to sup on your bones. Do you expect me to forget my appetite because it is not just?" ✺ "In a manner of speaking, yes," the Brahmin said with a shiver. ✺ "Brahmin, you are more foolish than I thought," said the tiger. "It is not the way of the world. But I shall give you a chance," continued the tiger. "Go from here and ask the first three things you meet what I should do with you.

Then return to me with the answers and I will follow the advice." ✺ So the tiger set the Brahmin free. As the Brahmin shook the dust from his robe, the tiger warned him: ✺ "Remember, the first three things you meet. And return quickly for I am getting hungrier by the minute…Do not make me come searching for you."

ow, the Brahmin was certain that his good deed would not end in his being eaten. It would not be just. So he set his face, serene and untroubled, towards the task at hand. ✿ The first thing he met was an elephant. Obeying the tiger's command to the

that he would not eat me, but when I freed him he wanted to eat me. Tell me then," asked the Brahmin. "Dost thou think the tiger ought to eat me?" ✿ "Since I was a calf my master has bound me with this iron ring around my leg," said the elephant. "I can go nowhere I want because he keeps me chained. When my master rides me, he beats my back with a cane so that

I will walk faster. I am a miserable servant to his every order."

✿ "I am sorry for your servitude, elephant," said the Brahmin. "However, my question was what dost thou think the tiger should do with me?" ✿ "Is it not plain to you what I think?" said the elephant. "We must obey the orders of our masters. The tiger is your master. Face your fate and be eaten." ✿ The elephant's answer deeply troubled the Brahmin and made him sad of

letter, he told the elephant of his ordeal. ✿ "I heard the tiger wailing under the mango tree and he asked me to free him. He promised me

heart. ✿ "Surely pity and compassion must exist in this world," said the Brahmin. ✿ So he continued to walk.

The next thing the Brahmin encountered was the pipal tree. The Brahmin told the pipal tree his story. ✱ "Tell me," asked the Brahmin. "Dost thou think the tiger ought to eat me?" ✱ "What have you to complain about, Brahmin?" replied the pipal tree. "I give shade and shelter to everyone who passes by. And what kind of gratitude do they show me? They tear down my branches to feed their cattle." ✱ "I am appalled by the way thou art abused," said the Brahmin. "But what about my predicament?" ✱ "Don't whimper," admonished the pipal tree. "Be a man. Go back to the tiger. The world is a cruel place." ✱ The Brahmin was astonished by the pipal tree's point of view. He grew greatly saddened.

But all was not lost. He saw a water buffalo in a field turning the wheel for a well. The Brahmin told the water buffalo his story. ✺ "Tell me," asked the Brahmin. "Dost thou think the tiger ought to eat me?"

✺ "You are a fool to expect gratitude," said the water buffalo. "Look at me and my life. When I once gave milk they fed me tender cotton-seed and delicious oil-cake. But now that I am dry they yoke me here and give me garbage to eat. Is that gratitude? There is no gratitude in this world. Go to your tiger. In his jaws awaits his only gratitude for you, Brahmin."

The Brahmin left the water buffalo and began his journey back to the tiger. The first three things he saw testified that he was to be the tiger's dinner. His fate had been decided. Surely, his life had been for naught, the Brahmin thought as he walked. ✲ He had spent his many years doing good turns for the people in his village, bestowing charity on all things great and small. He studied the holy books of India and extracted meaning. What a fool he had been to think that he was a wise man and understood the ways of the world. ✲ "I am nothing more than the tiger's dinner," said the Brahmin with pain and suffering in his voice.

✲ "Excuse me, holy one," said a voice from behind the Brahmin. "What is this you speak about? You want to eat the tiger for dinner?"

✲ The Brahmin turned to see who it was that spoke to him.

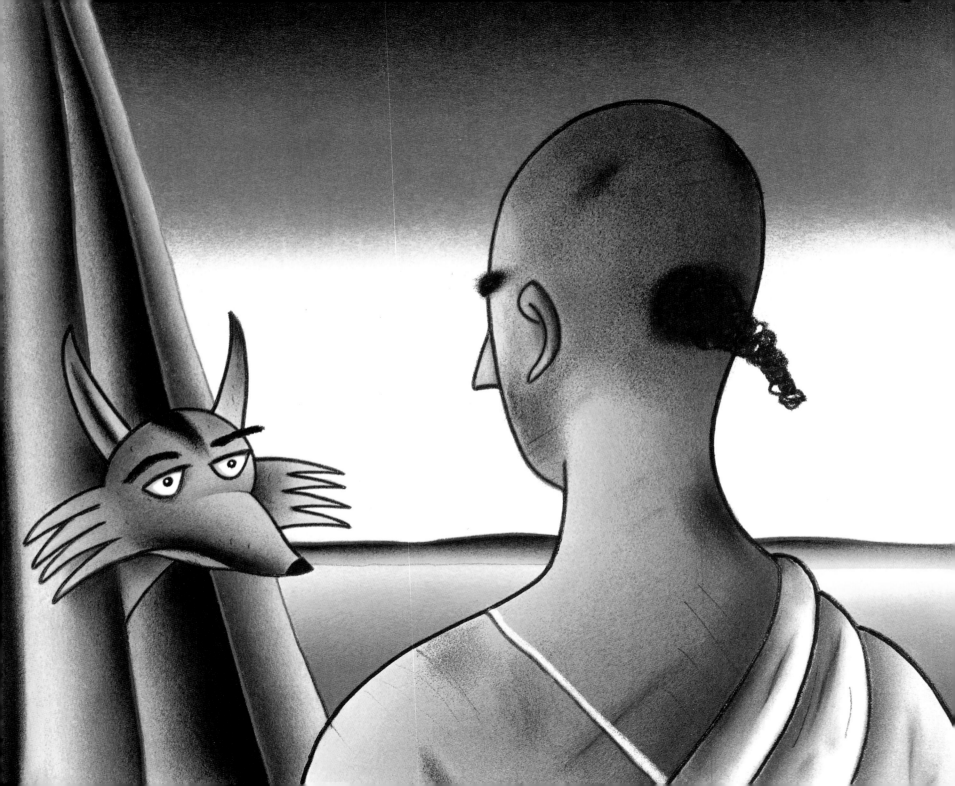

There he saw a jackal. ✸ "No," said the Brahmin. "I do not want to eat the tiger for dinner. The tiger will eat me for dinner." ✸ "But that is strange," said the jackal. "Does not the tiger know that the meat of the holy men is always tough and full of gristle?" ✸ "That is beside the point," the Brahmin said sadly. "I freed the tiger from a cage and now he wants to eat me." ✸ "That is most problematical," said the jackal. "But tell me, holy one, why did you free him from the cage?" ✸ The Brahmin was getting weary of this jackal and all his questions. ✸ "Before I let the tiger out of the cage, he promised that he would not eat me," said the Brahmin. ✸ "Brahmin Babu," said the jackal, scratching his head. "This is most confusing to me. I must sit down and decipher this conundrum."

The jackal sat on the road to think. He crossed his legs and put his chin in his paws. He grew deep in thought. Suddenly a look of confusion overcame the jackal's face. ✪ "Pardon me, holy one," said the jackal. "This is quite perplexing. Would you mind explaining it to me once again?" ✪ So the Brahmin again told the story of the tiger in the cage and how he freed the beast . And when he came to the part where the tiger wanted to eat him, the jackal shrieked. ✪ "Yeee-oow. There it goes again," cried the jackal. "I simply can't understand. The story seems to go in one of my ears and out the other." ✪ "I have decided," said the jackal. "Take me to the place where this most unfortunate event occurred. I will better understand it there."

nd so the Brahmin and the jackal went to the tiger, who lay in front of the cage sharpening his teeth and claws.

❁ "It is about time, Brahmin," the tiger roared. "You have kept me waiting for our dinner."

❁ "Our dinner," said the Brahmin, as his knees knocked together and his teeth chattered. "It is a most delicate way you have spoke it."

❁ "Come, Brahmin," growled the tiger. "Let us begin eating."

❁ "One moment please," said the Brahmin. We have a most curious visitor who insists on certain knowledge. Quite frankly, his persistence is getting under my skin."

❁ "It seems that I've explained my situation to him and he is unable to understand," said

the Brahmin. "So before our dinner, I thought I could better show him with you and the cage before us." ❁ The Brahmin went to the tiger and whispered, "This will not take long: the

jackal is dimwitted and certainly it would not be just to brush him aside." ❁ The tiger groaned and begrudgingly consented to the request.

So the Brahmin began to tell the story once again. The Brahmin did not miss a single detail, spinning the very longest of yarns. ✿ "Oh, my poor brain," squealed the jackal, squeezing his head with his paws. "Oh, my poor brain. I simply cannot understand the particulars of this tale." ✿ The tiger rolled his eyes back into his head. Surely this jackal lacks cleverness, the tiger thought. ✿ "Let me see if I have this correctly," continued the jackal. "The Brahmin was in the cage, and the tiger came walking by." ✿ "No, you fool!" roared the tiger. "I was in the cage. Is your head filled with camel dung?" ✿ "Oh, yes Sire," said the jackal, trembling with fright. "I have a most tremendous amount of camel dung in my head. Now I think I understand the story." ✿ So, the jackal continued with yet another version of the tale: "The tiger and the Brahmin are in the cage together. And the tiger comes walking by. Ah, but wait! How can the tiger be in the cage and outside the cage at the same time? One cannot occupy two places in space simultaneously. Surely, that is axiomatic!"

The tiger was getting angrier by the second. Clearly, this jackal was a lunatic and he was delaying the tiger's dinner. ✿ "You idiot!" bellowed the tiger. "How can you be so stupid, jackal?" ✿ "Don't mind me, Sire," said the jackal to the tiger. "Begin your dinner, for I shall never understand." ✿ "Yes, you will understand!" the tiger raged. "I will make you understand. Look–here, at me. I…am…the…tiger." ✿ "Yes, Sire," replied the jackal. ✿ "And that…is the cage." ✿ "Yes, Sire." ✿ "I was in the cage," said the tiger. "Understand?" ✿ "Yes, Sire,…I mean, no, Sire, I mean…what do you mean, Sire?" ✿ "I mean I was in the cage," said the tiger. ✿ "But how did you get in the cage?" asked the jackal. ✿ "Why, the usual way of course," hollered the tiger. ✿ "Oh, it is my head again," wailed the jackal. "I just cannot seem to understand it. Please do not be angry with me, Sire. Just answer: What is the usual way?"

The tiger had finally lost what little patience he possessed. So he jumped into the cage and declared, "This way, you fool! Now, you understand now?" ✺ "Perfectly," said the jackal. And no sooner had the word left his mouth than the jackal shut the door of the cage, trapping the tiger once again. ✺ "Now," said the jackal to the Brahmin. "If you permit me to say so, I think we shall leave the tiger in the cage this time!" ✺ The Brahmin looked on in awe.

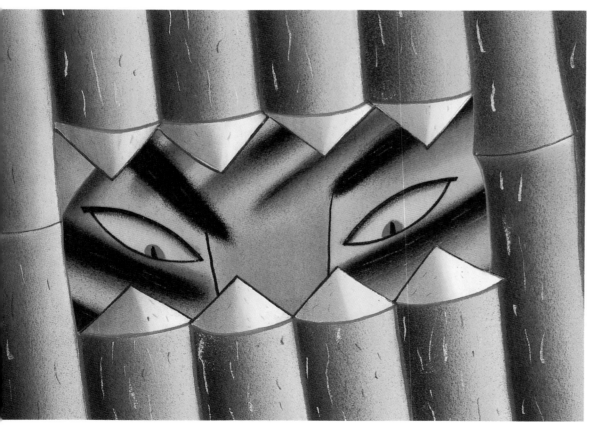

ree me at once!" ordered the tiger. "You cannot leave me here, holy one." ✲ "I have pity for you, tiger," said the Brahmin. "Perhaps when you are a Sahib's rug you will learn gratitude. And now I bid thee farewell." ✲ So the Brahmin and the jackal left the tiger in the cage, still screaming for mercy. ✲ "You are most clever," said the Brahmin to the jackal. "You have taught me a lesson that I never found in my holy books." ✲ "You flatter me, holy one," said the jackal. "Now I must go." ✲ And with that the jackal left the Brahmin, and scampered down the road out of the village.

As for the Brahmin, he continued studying the holy scriptures and acquiring merit by helping all things great and small. But he lived the rest of his life a much wiser man. As a result of the cleverness of the jackal and the deceit of the tiger, the Brahmin had learned the ways of the world.

❈ For in India, all things have a purpose.